The Clatterbangs Go To The Zoo

By Neil Gaw

Illustrated By Jose Ohi

The Clatterbangs were awful
The worst people you could find

Rude, noisy and terrible
Not one bit of them was kind

Four of them altogether
There was the Father and the Mother

Kerry was their daughter
And Jerry, her little brother

Kerry had many awful habits
But her favourite was
picking her nose

She loved to while away the hours
Digging for those green crows

And last but not least was Jerry
A mischievous little critter

He let his dog poop wherever it wanted
And thought nothing of dropping litter

One sunny day The Clatterbangs
Were all clatterbanging about

Jerry and Kerry were fighting
Then Father began to shout

"Now where are those slimy snails
I want to stomp them with my boots"

But the snails heard him clatterbang about
And they were in cahoots

But one furry fella had seen her coming
And filled his hands with mud

He flung the muck into her face
"Why is your aim so good??"

Jerry found the tiger's cage
And prepared his nose and tongue

"I'll scare that overgrown cat so much!"
But he couldn't have been more wrong

And so their day had ended
They got home tired and sad

"Perhaps all this wouldn't happen to us
If we weren't so very bad ... "

The Clatterbangs Go To The Zoo

By Neil Gaw

ISBN: 9781077168374

Look Out For Other Books In The Clatterbang Series!

44029743R00016

Printed in Poland
by Amazon Fulfillment
Poland Sp. z o.o., Wrocław